THE BARGAIN

adapted by Bob Read from
Francis Greig's original story

HANDLE WITH CARE

Bob Read

Published in association with the
Adult Literacy and Basic Skills Unit

Hodder & Stoughton

A MEMBER OF THE HODDER HEADLINE GROUP

All illustrations, including cover illustration,
by Graham Humphreys

British Library Cataloguing in Publication Data

Read, Bob
   Bargain AND Handle with Care. –
   (Spooked! Series)
   I. Title   II. Read, Bob   III. Series
   428.6

   ISBN 0-340-59032-7

First published 1993
Impression number   11 10 9 8 7 6 5 4 3
Year   1999 1998 1997 1996 1995

The Bargain is adapted by Bob Read from the original story, *The Bargain*, by
Francis Greig, first published by Jonathan Cape Limited, 1981,
copyright © Francis Greig 1981.

Printed in Great Britain for Hodder & Stoughton Educational,
a division of Hodder Headline Plc, 338 Euston Road, London NW1 3BH
by St Edmundsbury Press Limited, Bury St Edmunds, Suffolk.

THE BARGAIN

1

'This can't be right, can it?'

'What?'

'Just here, look.'

Andy put a ring in pencil round the advert.
He folded over the newspaper and gave it to Simon.

'You mean this ad for the Escort?' Simon asked.

'Yes. Just read it.'

'Escort XR3i ... K reg ... ' Simon stopped reading
and looked up at Andy. 'Are you mad?
We're looking for a cheap second-hand van.
Not a K reg XR3i!'

'I know that, but I happened to see this as well.
Just read on. You'll see why,' Andy said.

'... Red ... In excellent condition ... 7000 miles ...
£10 or near offer ... ' Simon stopped and looked up
at Andy again. He laughed and said, 'It's a joke.
Or a misprint. They must have left a few noughts
off. It should have been ten thousand.'

'That's what I thought,' Andy said.

'Of course it's a misprint,' Simon said. 'You didn't think someone was getting rid of a K reg XR3i for a tenner?'

'Well, no. Not really.'

'What do you mean, "Not really"?' Simon asked. 'Do you know how much they cost new?'

'Yes. About thirteen or fourteen thousand,' Andy said.

'Right then,' said Simon. 'It must be a misprint. Still, I suppose there will be a lot of crazy people like you who will still ring him up. The poor bloke will have to take his phone off the hook for a week!' Simon found the idea so funny he was almost shouting.

'OK. OK. Keep you voice down,' Andy said, looking round at the other people in the cafe. He reached over the table for the newspaper and read the advert to himself again. Simon finished his cup of tea.

Andy kept thinking about the advert. He had always wanted an XR3i. It was the sort of car he dreamed about getting if he ever won the pools. He said, 'Perhaps there's a reason for it. Perhaps the bloke did it for a bet with his mates. If no one rings up about it, he wins the bet. If anybody does ring up, he has to sell it.'

'That's stupid, Andy. No one would take on a bet like that,' Simon said. 'If you ask me, it sounds like a set-up for one of those Candid Camera stories. Didn't you see any adverts for vans?'

'No ... I didn't, as it happens,' Andy said.
His mind was still on the Escort. 'I could just ring the number. There's a phone on the wall over there. It wouldn't do any harm,' Andy said.

'Go on then. Perhaps after that we can get on with finding a van,' Simon said. 'Could you get some more tea on your way back as well?'

Andy stood up and walked to the phone.
Simon called out to him, 'See if you can knock him down a bit. Offer him a fiver!'

2

Andy rang the number. He put one hand over his ear
to block out the noise of the cafe. He hated ringing
up about cars. It seemed such a game, he thought.
You could never believe what people said.
Even people who were normally very honest
seemed to think it was OK to lie to you when selling
their car.

Perhaps Simon was right as well. This one would be
a waste of time. He was just about to hang up when
someone answered the phone.

'Jane Dashwood ... hello?'

Andy wasn't sure how to begin. She sounded posh.
Funny how you can tell that from just three words,
he thought. 'I'm ringing about the ad in the paper.
The red Escort ... '

'Oh, yes,' the woman said.

Simon waited for her to carry on, but there was just
silence.

'Is it ... ' Andy began, 'I mean, has it gone?'

'No. As a matter of fact, it hasn't. You are the first
person to call, to tell you the truth.'

Andy did feel she was telling the truth as well.
That was a change, he thought.

'It's an XR3i, isn't it? K reg, with about 7000 miles on the clock?'

'That's right,' the woman said.

'And you're asking ten pounds for it?'

'That's right.'

'I hope you don't think I'm being ... well, I mean, is there anything wrong with it?'

'Nothing so far as I know. It's my husband's car actually, but I know he has looked after it.'

'It hasn't been in an accident or anything?' Andy asked. There must be a catch somewhere, he thought.

'Goodness me, no. Nothing like that, I can assure you.'

Andy felt she sounded a bit offended. She wasn't used to selling cars, that was for sure. Still, he would have to ask the vital question.

'Do you have the registration papers and everything ... ?'

'Yes, of course. What are you trying to imply?' The woman sounded angry.

'I'm sorry ... I didn't mean ... It's just that ... ' Andy said.

'Well, would you like to come and see the car or not?'

'Yes, of course. I could come over now, if that's OK with you.'

'That's fine then.' The woman did not sound so angry now. 'The name of the house is Woodlands. It is just off Park Road. It's set back a bit from the road. Look out for two tall beech trees and you can't miss it. There's one either side of the drive-way gate, Mr ... I'm sorry, I didn't catch your name.'

'Er ... ' Andy was thinking that he did not know what a beech tree looked like. 'James. My name is Mr James. I'll be there in about half an hour.'

'I look forward to seeing you then, Mr James.'

Andy walked back to the table.

'You forgot the tea,' Simon said.

Andy was not listening. He was looking down at the advert in the paper. He was going over and over what the lady had said on the phone.

'Are you feeling OK, Andy?' Simon asked. 'You look a bit pale.'

'It sounds too good to be true,' Andy said.

'It's a joke of some sort. It has to be,' Simon said.

'But she sounded so posh, you know. Not the type to get involved in practical jokes. Anyway, I'll have to go. She's expecting me in half an hour.'

Andy stood up to leave.

'Are you sure you know what you're doing? You don't seem yourself,' Simon said, as Andy started to walk towards the door.

At the door Andy turned and called back, 'Yes. I'm OK. By the way, you don't happen to know what a beech tree looks like, do you?'

Simon just shook his head. Andy's definitely not himself today, he thought.

———————

3

Andy left his motorbike at the corner of Park Road.

It was a wide quiet road. The houses here were worth a lot of money. They were all set back quite a way from the road, with long smooth lawns like bowling greens.

Andy didn't know the area well, but he remembered coming along here when he had his first driving lessons.

My instructor will have a shock if he sees me driving an XR3i, he thought.

It was not difficult to find 'Woodlands'. There was a name plate on the gate post. As Andy walked through the drive-way gates, he looked up at the two trees that formed an arch high over his head.

So that's what beech trees look like, Andy thought.

He saw a man sweeping up leaves into neat piles on the lawn.

'Are you Mr Dashwood?' he asked.

'No, I'm just the gardener. If it's Mrs Dashwood you're looking for, you'll find her up at the house.'

This is some house, thought Andy.

As he walked up to the front door, a tall woman in a pale blue dress came out from around the side of the house. She held out her hand and said, 'Hello. You must be Mr James. My name is Jane Dashwood.'

'Yes, I've come about the car.'

'I was just getting it out of the garage for you. If you would like to come this way?'

She was younger than Andy had expected, about thirty perhaps. As they walked around the side of the house, Andy saw the Escort standing outside the garage on the drive.

It was a beautiful car. The bright red bodywork gleamed in the sunshine. There's not a mark on it, Andy thought, as he walked towards it. It was so beautiful that he suddenly saw that Simon was right. It had to be a joke. He still could not understand it, but it had to be a joke. A car like this was worth thousands.

Still, he might as well sit in it, he thought. He did not often have the chance to get behind the wheel of an XR3i. He put his hand on the door handle and looked back at the woman in blue. 'May I?' he asked.

'Yes, of course. The papers you asked about on the phone are in the glove compartment, Mr James.'

Andy got in and started the car. The engine sounded quiet but very powerful. Andy sat for a while looking around the inside of the car. This is a beautiful car, he kept thinking. He switched the

engine off and stepped out into the sunshine.
As he gave the car keys back to the woman in blue,
he did not quite know what to say.

'What do you think, Mr James?'

'It's beautiful,' Andy said.

'I would let you take it for a test drive, but I'm
afraid I have an appointment in ten minutes.'

'That's OK, Mrs Dashwood. I understand.'

Andy did not know what to say next. He felt silly
and expected her to start laughing at any moment.
In fact, she looked a little embarrassed. There was a
moment's silence.

'I'm sorry if you think me a little pushy, but do you
want to buy the car, Mr James?'

'Well, yes, of course, but I ... '

'Did you bring the money?'

'You mean the ten pounds? Yes. It's here,' Andy
said, taking the two five-pound notes from his
pocket. He could not believe this was happening.

'Thank you, Mr James. I was sure you would like
the car, so I wrote out a receipt before you came.
I have a copy for you and a copy for me. If you
would just sign them both here?'

She held out a pen to Andy. Andy signed them both,
still in a daze. He handed them back to the woman.

'Thank you,' she said. 'I hope everything is in order.'

She took the two five-pound notes and gave Andy his receipt.

Andy looked at the receipt and then looked up at the woman in blue.

'But this beautiful car ... for ten pounds? This is crazy. How can you do such a thing?' Andy said.

'I wondered when you would ask. But don't worry, Mr James. It's all legal and above board.'
She slipped the money into a side pocket in the blue dress.

She then went on, 'You see, my husband left me three weeks ago. I found out he was having an affair. The next day he ran off with her. Then last week he wrote and asked if I could send his clothes and belongings to his office in London. He also asked if I could sell his car and send him the money.'

She tapped the pocket in her blue dress and smiled, 'He won't get many candle-lit dinners out of this, will he, Mr James?'

HANDLE WITH CARE

1

'He's dead, Alan. You've gone and killed him.'

'What do you mean – dead?'

'What I say. Dead.'

'Are you sure, Frank?'

'Of course I'm sure. Just look at his eyes.'

Alan looked at his eyes. He looked dead all right.

'What are we going to do, Frank?'

'What are *you* going to do, more like.
You killed him, Alan,' Frank said and laughed.

'Come on, Frank. It was only an accident.
You saw what happened.'

'There's no point going on about that now, Alan.
He's dead now, and you killed him. I told you to be
extra careful, as this was your first job. But, no, you
wouldn't listen, and now look what you've gone and
done.'

Alan shook his head. He just couldn't believe what
had happened. It had all happened so quickly.

'Do you think people will notice?' Alan asked.

'What?' Frank said.

'Do you think people will notice that he's dead?'

'Are you crazy? Will anyone notice? Of course they'll notice he's dead!'

Alan looked at Frank. Then he looked down at the body. Frank was right. Anyone could tell he was dead.

'What am I going to do, Frank? I don't know how to handle something like this. This is my first job.'

'You don't have to tell me that!'

'Come on, Frank. Don't be like that. Help me.'

'OK. OK. OK. Don't panic.' Frank said.

He rubbed his chin with his hand, and after a moment he began to smile. He looked up at Alan, tapped the side of his nose with his finger and winked.

'Just you trust your old mate Frank.'

He gave Alan a big smile.

'Everything's going to be OK.'

2

'Frank?'

'What?'

'I've been thinking.'

'It's a bit early in the day for you, isn't it?'
Frank said and laughed. He looked at his watch.
It was 7.30. It was time to open. He walked over to
unlock the door of the Red Star parcel office.

'I was thinking, Frank. Perhaps I should just go and
tell the station manager the truth. OK, so I pushed
the parcel trolley into a wall and a few boxes fell
off. But, well, how was I to know there was a
hamster in one of them?'

'It said so on the side of the box,' Frank said and
laughed. He walked back round the counter.
'Anyway, didn't you check your parcel list this
morning when you took the boxes off the train from
Norwich?'

'I did give it a quick look but I thought it said
"One brown hamper",' Alan said.

'What?' Frank asked.

'A brown hamper. You know, one of those cane
baskets you use for picnics and stuff. It felt a bit like
a hamper too, when I picked it up, really light,

if you know what I mean. Are you all right, Frank? What's up?'

Frank had turned away from Alan and walked into the yard. His shoulders were shaking. He was trying very hard not to laugh. Alan followed Frank out into the yard.

Out in the yard Frank burst out laughing.

'A brown hamper,' he kept saying. 'A brown hamper. That's brilliant, Alan! You'll be the death of me, young man.'

He laughed even louder.

'Then you'll have two bodies to get rid of!'

3

Out in the sunny yard Frank sat down on a bench to roll a cigarette. He was still smiling about Alan and the hamper. Alan sat down on the bench next to Frank. It felt good to be out in the sunshine.

Frank opened a new tin of tobacco. The inside of the tin lid flashed silver in the sunshine. The dark tobacco had a rich sweet smell Alan liked very much. He liked to watch Frank roll his cigarettes. Frank always took his time rolling a cigarette, as if he was giving a demonstration.

Frank had thick heavy hands, and it looked funny to see his big hands fussing with the little paper and the tiny threads of tobacco. He rolled the little cigarette between the fingertips of his two big hands, then held it up to his mouth. He ran the tip of his tongue along the edge of the paper. He looks like an animal nibbling something in his paws, Alan thought and smiled.

Then suddenly he stopped smiling. He remembered the dead hamster. He looked at Frank.

'What do you think then, Frank?' Alan asked quickly. 'Is it best just to own up and tell the manager?'

Frank nipped out some threads of tobacco from the end of the roll-up and put the cigarette in his mouth.

He took out his matches.

'You can if you like, Alan.'

He struck a match and held it to the cigarette in his mouth. His hands made a little cage around the match and the cigarette.

'But how would you feel about going back to white-washing the edges of the platforms, Alan, like you did in your first week? Because that's what it will mean, you know.'

Frank took a long drag on the cigarette. He tipped back his head and blew out a cloud of cigarette smoke. He looked at Alan. He could see Alan was worried. These youngsters just can't take a joke nowadays, he thought. Still, perhaps he had been a bit hard on him.

'Hey! Come on. Relax. Just do as old Frank says, Alan. My plans always work. You'll be OK.
This will be a great story to tell your mates down the pub! Come on. What about it?'

Alan did not know what to do. Frank seemed to think the accident with the parcel trolley was quite serious. He did not want to lose his new job in the parcels office. But, on the other hand, he could not believe that Frank's plan would work.

'Come on, Alan. You're running short of time.
The customer is expecting the parcel at ten.'

'OK, Frank. You win. What do I do first?'

4

It did not take Alan long to ride into town on his motorbike. But time was beginning to run out, he thought, as he rode past the church down to the High Street.

He looked at his watch. It was nine o'clock. Alan worked out he had about twenty minutes to buy another hamster just like the other one and then get back to the station.

Alan pulled into a supermarket car-park. He got off the bike and took off his crash helmet. He remembered the hamster had a patch of white under its chin. He must not forget that. Frank said he had to get a hamster that was exactly the same as the other one. It was brown, with little grey ears and a white belly.

Alan walked quickly across the sunny car-park. He could feel the black tarmac warm under his feet. A woman came by, pushing an empty supermarket trolley. The silver grill of the trolley shone brightly in the sunshine. Just like a big hamster cage, Alan thought. All he could think about at that moment was hamsters.

He walked out of the car-park and up the High Street. He wondered if the pet-shop would have the right sort of hamster.

Alan thought back to last week and to his first day at the station. The men in the stores had sent him out with a list of things to get. A glass hammer, a left-handed screw-driver and a tin of striped paint. He had not known it was all a joke until the girl in the DIY shop had told him.

Alan stopped outside the pet-shop. Thinking back to last week in the DIY shop had made him even more nervous. He pretended he was reading the little adverts in the window. He would wait and go in when there was no shop assistant around this time. He always hated it when they came up to you as soon as you went into a shop. And today of all days he did not want to have to do any explaining.

The door of the pet-shop was half open. Alan could just see inside. One wall was full of cages. He could hear budgies and parrots. Water bubbled in fish tanks. There was the dry smell of sawdust and dog-biscuits. At the back he could just see a little card on a cage. It said 'Golden Hamsters'.

Great! Alan thought. And there were no shop assistants about either. Alan pushed open the door and went in.

5

'Can I help you?'

The girl's voice made Alan jump. She was kneeling down by a fish tank. After the sunshine outside it seemed dark in the shop. That was why he had not seen her. She stood up and smiled at Alan.

'Can I help you?' she asked again.

Alan was so surprised he just said the first thing that came into his head, without really thinking.

'I was looking for a hamster,' he said. 'A small brown hamster actually, with a white belly, little grey ears and a patch of white under the chin.'

'What's he done? Killed somebody?' the girl said and laughed.

'What?' Alan said.

'Sounds like you're from the police. You know, looking for someone on the run!' the girl said and laughed again.

'Oh, yes. I see what you mean,' Alan said. He smiled and laughed. He liked the girl's pretty blue eyes. As he laughed, he had an idea.

'Well, yes. It's for my sister actually. The thing is, I found her hamster dead in its cage this morning.

She's taking her A levels at the moment. I didn't want her to be upset, so I thought that if I got one that looked the same she wouldn't notice.
I was going to wait and tell her after the exams.'

'I see. That was kind of you,' the girl said.

Alan was amazed at himself. He had never lied to anyone like that before. He was amazed how easy it was. He ought to do it more often, he thought.
He seemed to be making a good impression on this girl with the pretty blue eyes.

The girl pointed at the cages at the back of the shop.

'If you'd like to come and look over here, I'm sure we can find one that will be OK.'

In five minutes Alan was running back to his bike in the car-park. In a little cardboard box he had a hamster that looked exactly like the other one.
He could not believe it had all gone so well.
He would just about make it back to the station in time to go out in the delivery van with Frank.
Frank had been right after all. Everything was going to be OK.

———————————

6

Just before ten o'clock Frank and Alan loaded the
van and set off. Frank drove. Alan sat next to him in
the cab. On his lap he held the box with the hamster
cage inside.

Alan was thinking about the hamster. Frank had
been really pleased with the one he had bought.
But somehow Alan felt there was probably
something he had forgotten. He had been in such a
rush in the pet-shop. And somehow it had all
seemed too easy.

But, still, Frank seemed to think the new hamster
was perfect. It was the same colour. It was the same
size and everything. But then suddenly, it came to
him. He remembered what it was he had not asked
about.

'Frank. Stop. Listen,' Alan cried out. He felt sick
with panic. 'I forgot to ask whether it was a male or
a female hamster! Let's go back to the shop, Frank!'

'Come on. Don't be stupid, Alan. We can't do that.
Look, it seemed exactly the same as the other
hamster to me. Now just relax. Trust your old mate
Frank. Everything's going to be all right.
Anyway, it's too late now. We're there.'

Frank pulled up outside a row of terraced houses.

'Number 14, I think it said, didn't it? For a Mrs Cooper?'

'Yes. That's right,' Alan said, looking down at the box. He looked up at Frank.

'But Frank, what if it's a boy when it should be a girl? Or a girl when it should be a boy?
She'll notice. I know she will. Women seem to know about these things. I don't think it's going to work, Frank. I don't think it's going to work.
What are we going to do?'

'Come on, relax. We're just going to do exactly what I'd planned to do right from the start.
I suppose you want me to show you how it's done, eh? Come on then. Just you wait and see. She won't suspect a thing. She'll just be thrilled to bits to see her old hamster again. We might even get a tip,' Frank said, as he winked at Alan.

Frank and Alan got out of the van and walked up to number 14. A woman opened the door just as Frank was about to knock.

'Thank you. I've been expecting you,' she said quietly. She took the cardboard box and went in, leaving Frank and Alan on the doorstep.

Alan looked at Frank.

Frank looked at Alan.

'So much for the tip,' Frank said.

Suddenly there was a scream from inside the house. Alan looked at Frank in alarm.

'I told you, Frank. I told you she would notice something!'

The door opened. The woman held the cardboard box in her hands. The top was open.

'What's happened to my hamster?' she shouted.

'Nothing, love. Look. There it is, fit and well, running around in its little wheel,' Frank said.

'That's not my hamster! My hamster is dead. He died yesterday at the vet's. I asked them to send him back, so we could bury him here at home!'